Dear Parent:

Your child's love of reading starts here!

Every child learns to read in a different way and at his or her own speed. Some go back and forth between reading levels and read favorite books again and again. Others read through each level in order. You can help your young reader improve and become more confident by encouraging his or her own interests and abilities. From books your child reads with you to the first books he or she reads alone, there are I Can Read Books for every stage of reading:

SHARED READING
Basic language, word repetition, and whimsical illustrations, ideal for sharing with your emergent reader

BEGINNING READING
Short sentences, familiar words, and simple concepts for children eager to read on their own

READING WITH HELP
Engaging stories, longer sentences, and language play for developing readers

READING ALONE
Complex plots, challenging vocabulary, and high-interest topics for the independent reader

I Can Read Books have introduced children to the joy of reading since 1957. Featuring award-winning authors and illustrators and a fabulous cast of beloved characters, I Can Read Books set the standard for beginning readers.

A lifetime of discovery begins with the magical words **"I Can Read!"**

Visit www.icanread.com for information on enriching your child's reading experience.

For young readers
everywhere, may all your
dreams come true.
—K.S.L.

Dedicated to Tobi
and You!
—N.M.

Ty's Travels: Winter Wonderland
 For information address HarperCollins Children's Books, a division of HarperCollins Publishers, 195 Broadway, New York, NY, 10007.
www.icanread.com

Library of Congress Control Number: 2021953559
ISBN 978-0-06-308363-9 (trade bdg.)—ISBN 978-0-06-308362-2 (pbk.)

Book design by Rachel Zegar
22 23 24 25 26 LBM 10 9 8 7 6 5 4 3 2 1
❖
First Edition

SHARED
My First
READING
I Can Read!

Ty's Travels

Winter Wonderland

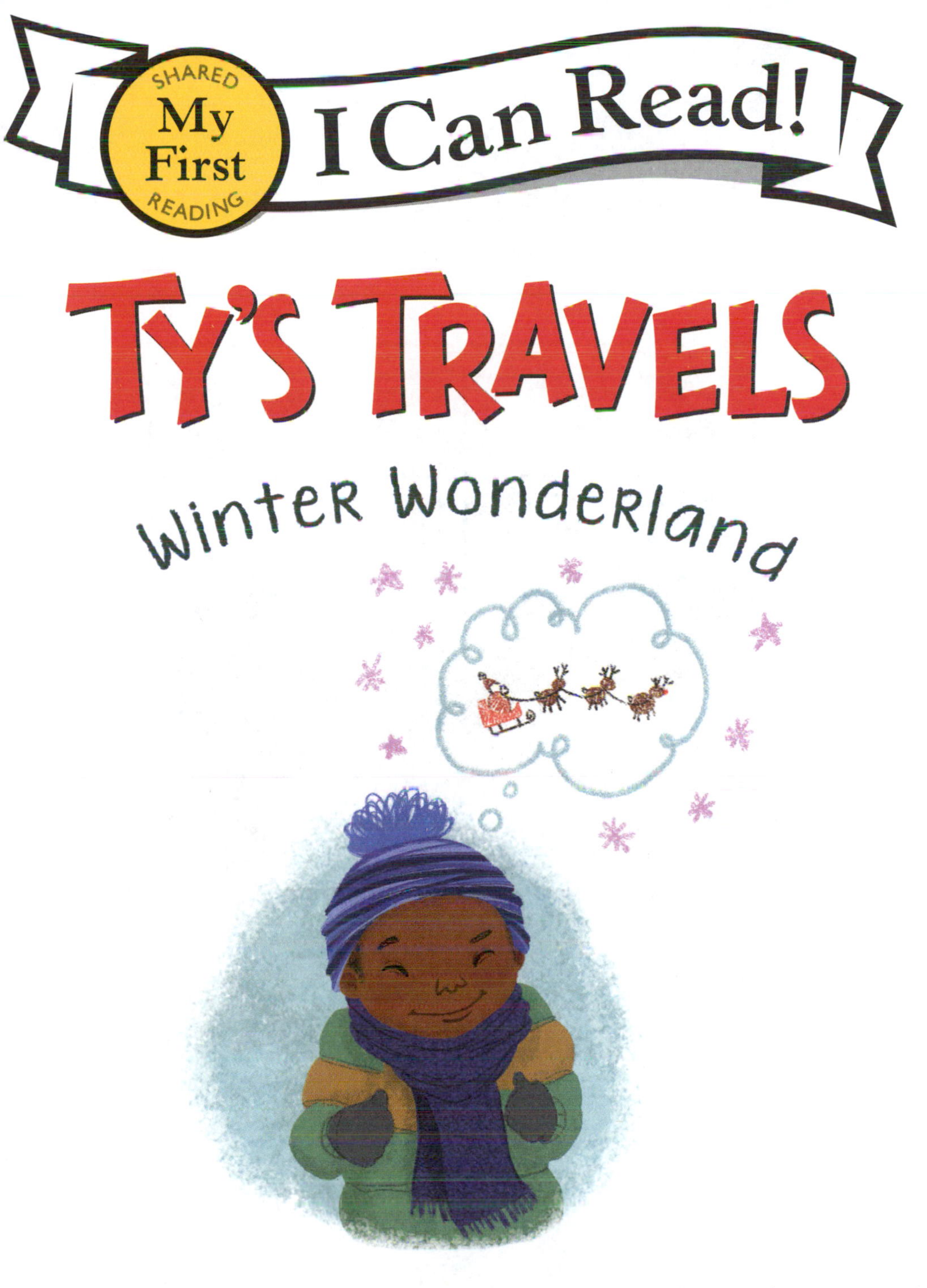

by Kelly Starling Lyons pictures by Niña Mata

HARPER
An Imprint of HarperCollins*Publishers*

Ty runs to the window.

He jumps up and down.
"It snowed! It snowed!"
Everything is wonderful.

Ty grins at what he saw.
It looked like his snow globe.
He gets his globe
and shakes it.

Snowflakes float down.
They cover the ground.
A sign says North Pole.

Ty runs upstairs.

“Can we go

to the North Pole?”

“Where?” Momma asks.

"The North Pole," Ty says.
"Better bundle up,"
Momma says.

Ty puts on his coat and hat.
He grabs his gloves and sled.
“Momma, it’s time to go,”
he calls.

Ty's dog, Brownie, wiggles.
Ty and Brownie can't wait!

When Ty and Mom step outside,
snowflakes float down.
Flakes cover the ground.

Ty, Momma, and Brownie are at the North Pole! Everything is wonderful.

north pole

The wind blows.
Snow twinkles in the air.
A snowpal waves at them.

Ty and Momma wave back.
Brownie barks hello.

“I hope we see Santa,”
Ty says.
“I don’t know,” Momma says.
“He’s pretty busy.”

They walk and walk.
Ty wishes and wishes.

"Look, Momma!" Ty says.
Christmas trees sparkle
and sway.
Polar bears sing.

Ty wishes and wishes.
But he doesn't see Santa.

Toy soldiers march.

Dolls dip and twirl.

Ty and Momma dance too.

Ty wishes and wishes.
But he doesn't see Santa.
Ty and Momma walk
to the park.

Ty shivers.

He puts his head down.

"Want to go home?"

Momma asks.

Ty is about to say yes.
Then he hears laughter.
Ty sees a hill.

Kids fly down like jets.

Whoosh!

Brownie barks and wiggles.
Ty grins and looks
at Momma.
She nods and smiles.

Ty and Brownie sled.

They fly down the hill.

Whoosh!

Snow twinkles in the air.
Ty hears jingle bells.
He sees reindeer and a sleigh.

Elves point to a workshop.

Ty's heart pounds.

He wishes and wishes.

Kids are lined up to meet . . .

Santa!

At home, Ty gets his globe.
He falls fast asleep.
Everything is wonderful.